# Jack and Jill

and

# Jack and Jill Go Skating

# Notes for adults

**TADPOLES NURSERY RHYMES** are structured to provide support for newly independent readers. The books may also be used by adults for sharing with young children.

The language of nursery rhymes is often already familiar to an emergent reader, so the opportunity to see these rhymes in print gives a highly supportive early reading experience. The alternative rhymes extend this reading experience further, and encourage children to play with language and try out their own rhymes.

**If you are reading this book with a child, here are a few suggestions:**

1. Make reading fun! Choose a time to read when you and the child are relaxed and have time to share the story.
2. Recite the nursery rhyme together before you start reading. What might the alternative rhyme be about? Why might the child like it?
3. Encourage the child to reread the rhyme, and to retell it in their own words, using the illustrations to remind them what has happened.
4. Point out together the rhyming words when the whole rhymes are repeated on pages 12 and 22 (developing phonological awareness will help with decoding language) and encourage the child to make up their own alternative rhymes.
5. Give praise! Remember that small mistakes need not always be corrected.

First published in 2008 by
Franklin Watts
338 Euston Road
London NW1 3BH

Franklin Watts Australia
Level 17/207 Kent Street
Sydney NSW 2000

Text (Jack and Jill Go Skating)
© Wes Magee 2008
Illustration © Melanie Sharp 2008

The rights of Wes Magee to be identified as the author of Jack and Jill Go Skating and Melanie Sharp as the illustrator of this Work have been asserted in accordance with the Copyright, Designs and Patents Act, 1988.

ISBN 978 0 7496 8018 3 (hbk)
ISBN 978 0 7496 8025 1 (pbk)

**Series Editor:** Jackie Hamley
**Series Advisor:** Dr Hilary Minns
**Series Designer:** Peter Scoulding

Printed in China

Franklin Watts is a division of
Hachette Children's Books
an Hachette Livre UK company.
www.hachettelivre.co.uk

# Jack and Jill

Retold by Wes Magee
Illustrated by Melanie Sharp

W
FRANKLIN WATTS
LONDON•SYDNEY

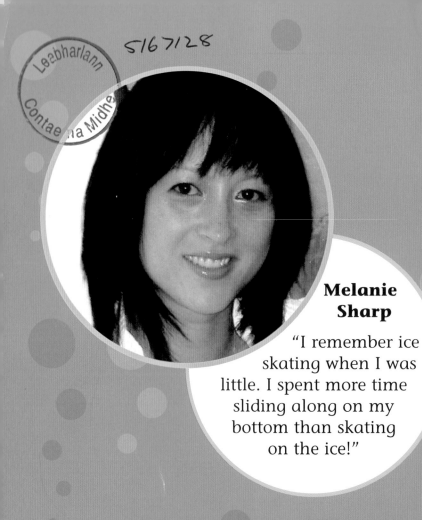

**Melanie
Sharp**

"I remember ice
skating when I was
little. I spent more time
sliding along on my
bottom than skating
on the ice!"

# Jack and Jill
# went up the hill,

To fetch a pail of water.

7

# Jack fell down,

8

# and broke his crown.

And Jill came tumbling after!

11

# Jack and Jill

Jack and Jill
went up the hill,
To fetch a pail of water.

Jack fell down,
and broke his crown.
And Jill came tumbling after!

Can you point to the
rhyming words?

# Jack and Jill
# Go Skating

by Wes Magee
Illustrated by Melanie Sharp

**Wes Magee**

"In winter, my pet cats love to slide across the frozen garden pond. They're clever! They always get to the other side without breaking the ice!"

Jack and Jill
went to the mill,

15

And skated
on the river.

17

# When they crashed,

the ice was smashed.

And now they shake and shiver!

21

# Jack and Jill
# Go Skating

Jack and Jill

went to the mill,

And skated on the river.

When they crashed,

the ice was smashed.

And now they shake and shiver!

Can you point to the
rhyming words?

# Puzzle Time!

Which clothes would you wear to go skating?

# Answers